MARC BROWN

ARTHUR'S SCIENCE FAIR TROUBLE

A Sticker Book

Random House ⌂ New York

www.stepintoreading.com

Educators and librarians, for a variety of teaching tools, visit us at www.randomhouse.com/teachers

Library of Congress Cataloging-in-Publication Data
Brown, Marc Tolon. Arthur's science fair trouble / Marc Brown. — 1st ed.
p. cm. — (Step into reading. A step 3 sticker book)
SUMMARY: Unable to think of an idea for a science fair project, Arthur borrows a model his father made in third grade but feels bad about it even before he gets into trouble.
ISBN 0-375-81003-X (trade) — ISBN 0-375-91003-4 (lib. bdg.)
[1. Science—Exhibitions—Fiction. 2. Honesty—Fiction. 3. Aardvarks—Fiction.]
I. Title. II. Series: Step into reading sticker books. Step 3.
PZ7.B81618 Arqe 2003 [E]—dc21 2002014887

Printed in the United States of America First Edition 10 9 8 7 6 5 4 3 2 1

STEP INTO READING, RANDOM HOUSE, and the Random House colophon are registered trademarks of Random House, Inc. ARTHUR is a registered trademark of Marc Brown.

On the first day of school,
Mr. Ratburn told his class
about the science fair.
"I want each of you
to do a science project.
On Parents' Night
the best project will get
a blue ribbon."

"I'm going to make a rocket
    for my project," said Buster.

"Oh, nuts!" said Arthur.

"That's what I was going to do."

"I'm sorry," said Buster.

"That's okay," said Arthur.

"I can think of something else."

Weeks passed.

Everyone had a project—

everyone but Arthur.

"I'm growing crystals.

They look just like diamonds,"

said Muffy.

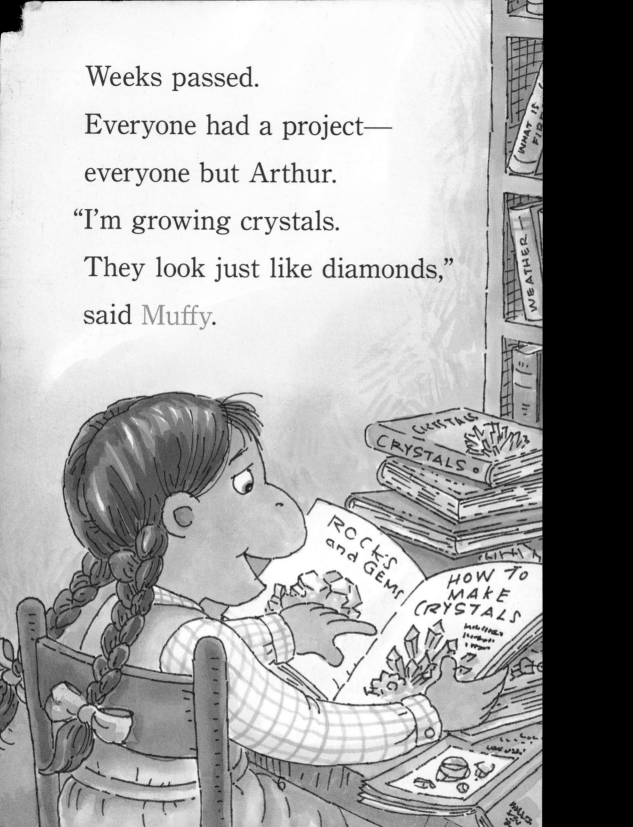

"I'm making a bird feeder
to study birds," said Francine.
"What are you doing, Arthur?"
"It's a secret," he said.

7

That night D.W. wanted
Arthur to play Go Fish.
"I can't," he said. "I have to think
of a science project for Monday!"
"The attic is full
of Dad's old projects,"
said D.W. "If you're smart,
you'll ask him for help."
"No help allowed," said Arthur.

After D.W. went to bed,

Arthur went up to the attic.

He looked in an old trunk

and found Dad's third-grade

science project.

It was a model of the solar system

with the sun and all nine planets.

But it was dusty and bent and

the planet Mars had fallen off.

Arthur had an idea.

Over the weekend
Arthur cleaned the model.
He glued Mars back in place.
He painted the sun orange.
He painted each of the planets
a different color.

13

Monday morning everyone
took their projects
to the lunchroom.
"Yours is the best,"
said Buster.

"Oh, no!" said Arthur.

"Oh, yes!" said Francine.

"I bet it gets the blue ribbon,"
said the Brain.

Suddenly Arthur felt sick.

All afternoon Arthur wanted
to tell Mr. Ratburn the truth.
After school Arthur said,
"I need to talk to you. . . ."
"Got to run. I'm late
for my dentist,"
said his teacher. "We can talk
tonight at Parents' Night."

Arthur ate his dinner slowly.

Very slowly.

"Hurry up," said his dad.

"We don't want to be late

for Parents' Night."

But they were late.
"And the blue ribbon
goes to Arthur Read,"
said Mr. Ratburn.
Now Arthur felt really sick.

"Amazing," said Dad.
"It looks like the project
   I did in third grade."
"It is the project you did,"
   said Arthur. "I just fixed it
   and painted it.
   I'm really sorry."
   Dad just shook his head.

"I think," said Mr. Ratburn,

"the blue ribbon should now go

to Arthur's father.

As for Arthur,

he has some explaining to do . . .

and a science project of his own."

D.W. said, "Oh, boy, Arthur,

you're in trouble."

And Dad said, "Arthur has to do
even more explaining
when we get home."
"Now you're in double trouble,"
said D.W.